THE DOCTOR'S OBSESSION

EMMA BRAY

CHAPTER ONE

Kevin

THE SUN IS GLINTING off the water of the Pacific Ocean, and the waves are crashing upon the shore, creating a soothing melody of peacefulness and tranquility — exactly what I need.

It's not easy being one of LA's top doctors. I work more than I sleep, and I practically live at the hospital.

Not that I'm complaining. I wouldn't have it any other way. If I can keep just one child from having to go through the type of pain that I did as a teen watching my mother slowly die before my eyes, then that makes it all worth it.

While treating patients is a primary part of my job and one that I love, I spend most of my time after hours in the lab, researching new medical finds, anything that I can use in my practice to benefit my patients.

But after years of working virtually nonstop, I've finally given in to my colleagues' prompting to take a well-deserved break.

I realize that I run myself ragged, but why shouldn't I? I'm a single guy. I live alone. I don't have any family to speak of. I have nothing to go home to, nothing holding me back from my career. There are so many people in need of treatment out there. I don't have time for breaks.

But what finally struck a chord with me was when one of my fellow doctors on staff at the hospital reminded me that I can't give my patients my best if I'm not healthy. And even I have to admit that the bags under my eyes have deepened over the past couple of months due to lack of sleep, and I'm practically staying awake on coffee—things that I would never advise my patients to do.

So now here I am. On a weeklong vacation that is proving more difficult for me than one of my more complex surgeries.

I sigh in frustration and scowl around at all the carefree people littering the beach.

I haven't relaxed in so long it's like I've forgotten how. I'm restless. It's hard for me to just lay in the sun and enjoy myself like everyone else on this beach. I feel like I should be doing something productive, something to save someone's life.

Do I have a God complex? I don't think it's that. I just hate being idle. I'm probably the only stupid son of a bitch alive who finds a vacation torturous. But it's true. I'd much rather be at the hospital working.

I heave a breath and gaze out over the water, my eyes taking in the people along the shoreline and those swimming in the ocean. They're so happy and carefree —two things that I'm not sure I can ever remember being.

My eyes rove in a steady line up the beach until they catch on a stunning girl with long sun-bleached hair. I take in the baby blue bikini she's wearing. The top is a bandeau style with a starfish embellishment right in between her breasts, and the bottoms completely cover a round little ass—the kind of ass that makes men salivate. It's not too big, yet it's got just enough shape to it to call to mind fruit ripe for the plucking.

Although she appears to have a petite frame, those shapely legs seem to go on forever. She's got to be wearing one of the most conservative bikinis out here today. She's certainly covering more of her body than the countless women strutting around the beach in thong bikinis and with their tits spilling out over undersized pieces of triangular fabric.

There's no shortage of eye candy on the beach for a man to enjoy today, yet my gaze is inexplicably drawn to her, and I can't help wondering why.

I can't remember the last time I really checked out a woman with this must interest. I've been living like a monk for years, too busy with my career to get involved in a relationship. Besides, I can take care of my needs on my own without the complication of a woman in my life, demanding time and attention I don't have to give.

But it's more than that, though. I'm just not into baseless sex and sleeping around just for the hell of it. Sure, when I was in college, I'd had my share of one night stands like every other guy, but I'd quickly found out that waking up next to a woman who meant nothing to me just wasn't my jam.

I haven't exactly sworn women off, but I haven't gone out of my way looking for them either.

I'm not one to sit on the beach ogling beautiful women, but something about this girl is different from the other beachgoers, and I stare at her, transfixed by the magnetism that seems to pull my gaze to her, wondering what it is.

A light breeze tousles her windswept hair, causing the ends of it to dance around her waist, and I feel a strange tightening in my chest.

I suddenly realize what's different about her. She's not smiling or laughing or frolicking like everyone else on the beach.

No, like me, she appears to be alone, and she's pensive, walking slowly along the shoreline, lost deep in her thoughts. Every now and then she stops and lifts her head to gaze out over the ocean.

I'm burning to know what she's thinking about. I want to see her eyes, but a pair of oversized glasses shields them from the sun and my probing gaze.

Despite her melancholy, she's a bright light, something pure and innocent shining from her. It's almost as if there's a halo of goodness and sweetness surrounding her, like she's an ethereal being set apart from the rest of us mere mortals.

I shake my head and run a hand along my jawline, forcing myself to stop staring at her—not like she's noticed. A quick glance around the beach shows several other males in the vicinity leering at her with undisguised looks of hunger on their faces, and a flash of irritation rolls through me.

It's irrational, but I want to punch the fuckers' lights out and then cover her up with my shirt and carry her off somewhere where we can talk and I can get to know her better.

When I can't deny myself any longer, I turn my eyes back toward her and see that she's waded out into the water. Now, I'm treated to the sight of the waves crashing against her legs and leaving her skin glistening with salty water droplets.

I frown as she continues to walk deeper into the ocean, the water reaching near the gentle swell of her breasts now. My eyes flick over to the yellow beach flag. It's just a medium hazard day with moderate surf and current. Still, I know better than anyone just how quickly one can lose control and get pulled under. I was a lifeguard in my younger days, and I've seen it happen too many times on yellow flag days people thought were safe.

I stand as an awful premonition of dread begins to grip me. She continues walking in up to her shoulders.

I'm standing poised on the balls of my feet, every muscle in my body alert and ready to race in after her at a moment's notice.

Another wave swells and crashes over her head.

I wait a beat. Then two. Then three.

Her head bobs up only to disappear again. Her arms flail.

I'm flying into the water before I can even fully process it.

I'm not fighting against the waves. I merely dive into them, attacking them with powerful strokes to reach her as quickly as possible.

She's so far out that by the time I finally reach her, her head isn't coming up anymore. Panic I've only known one other time—when my mom died—grips me.

No! No! My pulse races, and I can hear the blood roaring in my veins. I don't even know her, but I know that the world will have lost something infinitely precious if this girl dies. Dammit, I should have followed her into the water sooner.

I clutch her body next to mine and swim us into swallower water where I scoop her up and run with her to the shore.

Paying no heed to the onlookers who have begun to gather around to watch the commotion, I lay her gently out on the sand and begin performing CPR like I'm trained to do.

Open the airway. Tilt her head back slightly to lift her delicate little chin. Check for breathing. Oh god, she's not breathing. Flatten my hands on her chest, one on top of the other and press hard and fast. Pump, pump, pump. Pinch her nose and breath my life into her mouth until her chest rises. Again. Pump, pump, pump. Breathe. Pump, pump, pump. Breathe. C'mon.

The third time's the charm. Finally, she begins coughing, and I help her turn over to expel the water from her lungs.

She takes in deep, ragged breaths that are music to my ears.

When her head turns back to me and her eyes meet mine, it's like a punch to the gut. That's how intense my reaction to her is.

I'm the one who suddenly can't breathe. Her eyes are big and luminous and so fucking soulful my chest aches with it.

They're not the deep blue of the ocean's depths. No, they're a light baby blue, the color of the sky, and so soft I want to wrap myself up in them and never leave.

She begins coughing again. As if from afar, my ears begin to register the sound of cheering from the crowd that's gathered around us.

I look up to see EMTs pushing through the crowd. Someone must have called them, and I'm pleased with how quick their response time was.

However, knowing I'll be recognized by the medical staff, I duck my head and slip away as they approach. I already hear people bandying about words like "hero" and "savior," and I certainly don't want to be on the news being lauded as such. I already have too much notoriety as a savior in this city as it is—and a savior I certainly am not, though I try—god do I try—to save them all.

I glance back through the crowd at where the EMTs are already checking her vitals and asking her questions, and as much as it pains me to walk away, I do.

She'll be in good hands.

***

Chloe

Golden eyes burning brighter than the sun. They're the first thing I se when I open my eyes from my near-death experience.

His face crowds out everything else. I barely have time to register a strong jawline, lightly lined with stubble, and sandy brown hair carelessly tousled by the wind.

He looks like a god come down from Mount Olympus to rescue me. My very own Hercules sent to rescue me. No mere mortal could exhibit such masculine beauty.

But then my lungs burn with the need to cough, and I turn back to the sand and violently expell more water from my mouth.

By the time my coughing fit is over and I turn back around, he's gone. Vanished from thin air. Like a super hero or something. He was there one minute—just long enough to save my life—and then the next. he disappeared. Poof.

If it weren't for all the people still gathered around the beach to serve as proof that someone had indeed saved my stupid ass from drowning into the scary depths of the ocean, I would believe that I imagined him.

I'm still not entirely sure what happened. One moment I was walking deeper into the ocean, enjoying the soft sway of the water around me, and the next I was in over my head, pulled under by a mighty current that I couldn't fight no matter how hard I tried.

The ocean is a strong bitch, and I'm no match for her with my puny, diminutive frame. I'm barely five foot two, and though I've always been slender, it's not from working out or anything. In fact, I abhor working out. The only kind of exercise I get is unplanned exercise from walking or running to get from point A to point B.

After reassuring the EMTs that I'm fine and that I don't need to be carted off to the hospital, I get up and make my way through the remaining throng of people with an overly bright smile designed to hide the tears that are threatening to swim to the surface at any moment. I'm determined to get out of here before I become fodder for the nightly news. How humiliating would it be to be on the news for being stupid enough to go too deep into the ocean on a yellow flag day and almost drown?

I don't want to hang around and find out.

Of course, I don't really want to go home either. It pains me to be in that house all alone. That's why I've spent nearly every second of the past few months away from there as much as I can. When I'm not looking for a job, I'm walking the beach or walking aimlessly through the streets—anything to keep me from having to sit all alone in the home Mom and I shared all my life. It hurts too much to be there now that she's not here.

The tears that have been pricking my eyes the

entire walk home from the beach finally begin to spill over. Fortunately, the little cottage that is now mine isn't too far from the beach. While it's not exactly an oceanfront bungalow, it's only located a couple of blocks from beachside.

Mom had always been a beach bunny, so when she'd found the tiny place for sale before I was born, she'd nabbed it. It wasn't a huge house, but we didn't need much room for just the two of us, and its close proximity to the ocean that she'd loved so much—too much in the end—more than made it up for its small size.

Although it hurts to be in the home she'd loved so much without her, I don't think I could ever sell it. There are too many good memories attached to the place.

So, I hang on just hoping that someday soon the hurt will lessen enough that I can stand to be there longer than just the night to crash long enough to sleep.

By the time I open the front door, my mind is completely immersed in my mother's death again, and the tears are streaming down my cheeks, all thoughts of my handsome rescuer forgotten.

And it's just as well.

I certainly don't want to end up like my mother.

Kevin

I can't get her out of my head. Every time I close my eyes all I see is baby blue. Those eyes of hers are haunting me, and for the millionth time, I find myself wishing I had stayed long enough to at least learn her name.

I want to find her, but I don't have the first clue as to where to look. I've gone to the beach I rescued her from, hoping to run into her again, but I never do.

I could almost believe that she really was an angel sent down from heaven for just a day if only I was the type of guy to believe that type of stuff.

Unfortunately, I'm not the type to believe in that nonsense. No, I'm more of the realist type who knows that I'm just a stupid man who fucked up and let her slip through my fingers.

So I go on like before, day after day throwing myself into my work, though now it's for more than just to keep me busy and to save everyone I can. Now, it's to help keep my mind off of the beautiful little angel that I can never have.

I might can control my thoughts during the

daytime hours, but I can't control my subconscious or where my dreams go every night, though.

It would be just my luck that the one woman who garners my interest in years is as elusive as a mystical mermaid.

It's probably just as well.

CHAPTER TWO

Chloe

TODAY'S the first day of the rest of my life. No more moping around and dwelling on my mother's untimely death. As much as it hurts, I have to move on.

Since I still can't stand to be in the house for very long, I made sure I took the job with the longest hours I could find. After months of applying to jobs and getting no callbacks, suddenly I got three offers in a week.

I take a deep breath and look up at the huge hospital building in front of me. I'll be working reception at Peckerton Memorial in a position that's sure to keep me plenty busy.

It's not exactly what I want to do for the rest of my life, but it's a stepping stone. At least I'll be working in healthcare, and that can only count as experience, right?

I really want to be a mental health counselor, but I don't have the money to go to college and get the necessary bachelor's degree—not yet anyway.

I square my shoulders and begin walking toward the front door. But that doesn't mean I won't get my degree. I will. I'll just work my ass off and save as much money as I can until I can afford to pay my way. Sure, I could take out student loans and do it right now, but I don't want to get caught in the student loan debt trap and start my career out in the hole.

And there's no way I could ever sell the house. That's not an option.

I put on my best game face and smile broadly as I report to the HR office for training. I'm introduced to a kindly older woman named Martha who undertakes the arduous task of training me.

She's patient with me, and her motherly attitude almost causes me to choke up a few times throughout the day, only highlighting the loss of my own mother.

I brush all those types of thoughts away, though. I

can't be breaking down and crying on the job. It is what it is, and I can't change it. Mom is gone, and all I can do is carry on with my life the best I can.

The job entails more than enough to take my mind off things and keep me busy. Between answering phones, replying to emails, and performing patient intake, the hours fly by.

By the end of my shift, I'm physically and mentally exhausted, so much so that the prospect of going home just fills me with relief that I'll be able to sleep instead of the usual dread at being in the empty home without Mom.

I'm packing up to leave, grabbing my purse, when I suddenly feel a tingle start at the base of my spine like a sixth sense or something. It runs all the way up my neck, and goosebumps break out on my skin as I turn around and gasp, nearly tripping over my own two feet with shock as I'm assaulted by a pair of warm, golden eyes.

I'd remember those eyes anywhere. They're the eyes of my mysterious hero, my Hercules from that day on the beach all those weeks ago.

His hands reach out to steady me, saving me again —only this time from falling—and the touch sends electric shockwaves throughout my skin even through our clothes. His hands are big where they grip my waist. If he wrapped them around me, I'm certain he could almost touch them together.

He's tall, so tall that I have to lean my head back to look up at him as he towers over me. His sandy-colored hair is carelessly brushed back from his face, and there's a lining of stubble along his jaw.

I wonder if he remembers me, but then I get my answer when he speaks, his voice a deep, smooth rumble. "Turns out you need just as much saving on land as you do in sea."

My face burns with mortification, but then I see his teasing smile and realize he didn't mean anything offensive by the statement.

Still, I'm humiliated. Twice now I've made myself look like an idiot in front of this man. This incredibly handsome man who judging by his long white coat is a doctor.

Holy freaking moly. A doctor. My Hercules is a doctor.

"I'm fine," I answer, nervously taking a step back from him. He releases me and lets his hands fall from my face as I put distance between us.

"You're a doctor here?" I ask stupidly just to fill the awkward void of silence that's descended upon us and because I don't have a clue what else to say.

"Yes, Dr. Kevin Blake," he introduces himself. His

eyes haven't left me once, and I find myself wanting to squirm under his gaze. His gaze is burning, invasive, like he's looking deeper inside me than anyone has ever looked before.

And I'm sure I must be losing my mind because that makes no damn sense.

"And you must be the new hire..." he prompts me. At his questioning gaze, I realize that I've been standing here just staring up at him like an awestruck teenager or something. If possible, my cheeks turn even redder.

"Chloe," I tell him before swallowing. "Chloe Danes."

"Chloe," he repeats my name slowly, and my toes curl in my sensible sneakers at the sensual way he says my name. I've never really liked my name, but my god, I love the way it sounds dripping from his lips.

"Oh, um," I begin suddenly, "I never thanked you for, you know, saving my life that day..." I trail off. God, I'm making myself out to be an even bigger idiot.

He shrugs off my praise, telling me humbly, "I'm no hero, Chloe. No need to thank me. Just don't get in over your head again, okay?"

I nod up at him. "Okay, Dr. Blake." It's nice to finally at least know the name of the man who rescued me.

"Please, call me Kevin," he insists.

I bite my lip nervously and watch as his eyes zone in on the motion, darkening. "Okay, Kevin," I say hesitantly, and his eyes snap back up to mine.

He gives me a dazzlingly charming smile and hands me a file. "Do you think you have time to file the last one before you leave for the day? I hate to ask you. I'm sure you're ready to be off the clock."

"Oh, no," I rush to reassure him. "It's no trouble at all." I take the file from him, and his fingers brush mine in the transfer.

I peek up at him, and he's looking down at me with an expression I can't identify on his face, but it takes my breath away.

He opens his mouth to speak, but then we're interrupted when a nurse comes flying out of the ICU doors calling his name.

"Dr. Blake! Room 7 is coding," she tells him frantically.

His head jerks up and he hurries to follow her, already barking orders.

I exhale, letting out the breath I didn't even know I was holding.

Kevin Blake, the dangerously handsome man who saved my life and who I now know is a doctor.

Kevin

Christ, after weeks of thinking I'd never see her again, and then she just falls right into my lap at my workplace.

I'd been coming out to return a patient file. I could have simply placed it in the return bin and it would have eventually been filed away, but when I'd seen that waist-length sun-kissed hair and that slim build, my body had instantly been on alert.

I'd hardly dared to hope that it was really her. Maybe it was just someone with a similar body type. I'd had to get closer to find out for sure, and when she'd turned around and that shade of blue that's been haunting me for weeks had stared up at me in startled surprise, I'd damn near come in my pants.

That's right. Me. A thirty-year-old accomplished doctor had almost ejaculated on the spot at the excitement of seeing the object of my obsession in the flesh again.

Chloe Danes. I now have a name to go with the face.

And I'm feeling better knowing that she must be of legal age if she got a job working reception here at the hospital. We don't hire underaged workers for legal reasons. It makes me feel like less of a creep knowing how many times I've beat off to mental images of the girl from the beach not even knowing how old she was.

I run a hand through my hair as I log into our database and pull up Chloe's file. I hated having to leave her like that earlier, but a patient needed me. When the nurse came out with that message for me, all my training instinctively kicked in. I went into full-on doctor mode, my primary focus being on saving my patient. Fortunately, we were able to stabilize him.

Unfortunately, Chloe had slipped through my fingers again without me getting to ask her out.

So, now I'm reduced to drastic measures to learn more about her. I realize that I could wait until the next morning when she's back at work to ask her to have a cup of coffee or dinner with me, during which time I could learn about her like any other normal man.

But I'm not a normal man when it comes to her. I'm a man who's regretted letting her get away for the past three weeks and who can't wait a moment longer to find out everything he can about her.

I don't know why she obsesses me so, but she does. It's like some primal tug deep within my being that I can't ignore.

My eyes quickly scan over the screen.

Nineteen. Fuck, she's young. I'm eleven years older than her. Not quite old enough to be her father—unless I started super young, that is.

She lives on beachside. I quickly jot down the address and her phone number. Not like I plan on calling her or showing up on her doorstep and freaking her out, but I still have to know how to reach her.

I click out of the file and start heading for the garage.

I know damn well I shouldn't start stalking an employee and that's exactly what I'll be doing if I drive by her house.

But I fucking do it anyway.

Kevin

She lives in a cute little beach bungalow a couple of blocks from the stretch of the beach where I saved her.

I park my car as inconspicuously as I can down the street and stare at the door, silently willing her to open it so I can get a glimpse of her.

The window blinds are drawn, and while I wish they weren't so I could look in on her, I'm also pleased that she doesn't have them wide open like lots of people who live in town do so that any fucker could look in on her.

No matter that today I'm any fucker. I'm different, I try to justify to myself. I would never hurt her. I just want to protect her. Our fates are twined irrevocably together. Ever since that day when I breathed my life into her on the beach and she was reborn as a part of me, taking a bit of my soul into her body, she's been mine in my mind.

And I've been beating myself up for letting her get away.

But not anymore.

She'll never get away from me again.

CHAPTER THREE

Chloe

MY NIGHT WAS RESTLESS, my dreams haunted by golden eyes and skillful hands.

Yes, I did an internet search on Dr. Kevin Blake as soon as I got home. Turns out the good doctor is a cardiothoracic surgeon with an extremely high success rate. He has nothing but good reviews on all the doctor rating sites.

A doctor. No wonder he'd known exactly what to do to get me breathing again. Saving lives was his thing.

In the moments I've thought of him since my

rescue, I've imagined he was a lifeguard or something. Never a doctor.

As if I wasn't nervous enough about my new job, my anxiety has only increased tenfold knowing that there's a good possibility I could run into him again.

And run into him I do. No sooner do I arrive and get settled at my desk than he's standing there looming over me.

It's still early, and there aren't even any patients in the waiting room yet. In fact, there's no one in the area but me and him.

I swallow and look up at him. I don't know why he makes me so nervous, like my stomach is in a little ball and my legs have turned to jelly. It can't just be because he's handsome. I've been around handsome men before, and none of them ever affected me this way.

Maybe it's the fact that he saw me at my worst, at death's door, and he brought me back from there. There's something intimate about the fact that he breathed his life into me, like I'm now his creation or something.

All I know is that his golden eyes are the first thing I saw when I'd opened my eyes after being pulled back from the brink of death, and now every time I see them, they look like the other half to my soul.

And that scares the shit out of me. That's the kind of dangerous, fanciful thinking that ultimately got my mother killed.

I cannot go down the same path she did. I won't. I refuse to.

Still, I can't stop the pitter patter of my heart when he greets me.

"Good morning, Chloe." His golden eyes are glowing down at me with warmth and an intensity that makes my heart skip a beat.

"Good morning, Dr.—" he raises an eyebrow at me, and I quickly correct myself. "Kevin."

Do I imagine the way his eyes seem to soften when I say his name?

"I'm sorry about the abrupt way I had to leave yesterday," he says, his gaze trailing over my face as if he's trying to commit every detail of it to memory.

"Oh," I shake my head. "You never have to apologize for being a hero." I smile up at him sincerely before I rethink what I said and ask him tentatively, "Your patient did make it, right?"

"Yes," he assures me, "he did, but I'm no hero, Chloe." He frowns as he says that last bit as if he hates being referred to as such.

I study him. I don't get it. I thought most doctors had God complexes and liked to be regarded as saviors.

He seems just the opposite. It's more than humility, I realize. He acts like he detests being thought of in a heroic light.

"Is that why you left that day?"I ask him.

I see the surprise register across his face and immediately want to take back my question. It makes it sound like he was supposed to stick around after saving my life, like he owed me something, when really it was just the opposite. If anything, I owed *him*—my life to be exact.

He looks like he wants to say more to me, but just then, Martha comes in the door, greeting both me and Kevin with a warm good morning and a huge smile.

Kevin's eyes flick back down to find mine. "Have dinner with me later." It's an order, not a request.

My eyes widen as I try to decline. "Oh, no, I—"

He cuts me off with a look that's so intense it takes my breath away. His eyes are smoldering and commanding all at once. "I'll pick you up at seven," he tells me firmly.

He turns to walk away before I can utter any protest, and I stare after him dumbfounded before I realize that I didn't give him my address.

Kevin

I'm being a pushy prick, but I can't help it. When she started to decline my invitation to dinner, I panicked.

I couldn't accept no from her. I need some time alone with her away from work so I can at least talk to her.

And now here I am sitting outside her house ten minutes early looking like an over-eager teenager about to go on his first date.

But fuck I barely made it through my day in anticipation of tonight.

I get out of my Maserati and walk up the stone-lined walkway to her house. I knock on the door and stuff my hands into the pockets of my slacks as I wait for her to come answer the door.

My blood begins to hum beneath my skin when the door opens and she's standing there in a little black dress that comes down just above her knees. It has a cowl neck that swoops down to show the tiniest hint of cleavage, and when she turns around to grab her purse, I see it plunges down to reveal a generous expanse of slender back. Her hair is piled up on her head so as not to obscure the view of the back of the dress, and I have to fight the insane urge to free the locks and watch them tumble down to cover her naked back from other male eyes.

Christ almighty, she looks good enough to eat. Fuck dinner. I can just feast on her all night.

"You look breathtaking," I tell her and watch with pleasure as her cheeks pinken at the compliment. I can think of many other ways I could make her blush, but I make a conscious effort not to let my thoughts go there. I'm already half hard in my boxer briefs, and it's taking everything in me to keep myself from hardening to full mast and embarrassing myself here on this residential street.

She's that damn gorgeous and tempting.

I take her hand and begin leading her to my car. I can't help noticing how my hand dwarfs hers. Her fingers feel so delicate in my grasp.

"How did you know where I live?" she asks me, shooting a skeptical look my way.

I wait until I get her settled in the passenger seat of my car and go around and put the car in drive before I answer her.

"I looked at your employee file," I admit.

I hear her tiny gasp and glance over at her to find her regarding me warily. "You went through my file?" she asks.

I nod. I'm not going to lie to her. Besides, all my

cards will be on the table soon enough, so there's no point in trying to hide my obsession from her. "Don't worry," I give her a reassuring smile. "I'm not a psychopath or something, and I certainly don't mean you any harm."

She's still looking at me like she half expects me to tie her up, so I try to lighten the mood with, "I saved your life, remember? Why would I do that if I planned on harming you?"

She grins and lets out a nervous laugh before her shoulders relax and she melts back into the seat.

I tighten my hands on the steering wheel as I imagine her body melting back into mine that way. How can I be jealous of a damn seat? I want her sitting in my lap, and I want to feel her melting back against my chest as my arms wrap around her, anchoring her to me and never letting her go.

"Kevin," she says my name hesitantly, and I glance over at her. "I'll be honest," she goes on, "I don't really understand what we're doing here."

"What is it you want with me?" she asks me frankly, twisting her hands in her lap.

"You'll understand everything soon enough. I promise," I tell her. I hate to be cryptic, but I can't tell her everything here where she's liable to bolt.

She gives me that wary look again.

I pull up outside my favorite Italian restaurant in the city and rush over to help her out of the car before the valet can do it. It's illogical, but I don't want another man's hands even touching hers. It's insane how territorial and possessive I already am of this girl.

I hand my keys to the valet to park and see the young boy's eyes light up at the prospect of getting to drive my Maserati. Good. I'd rather him be fixated on the car than Chloe, who is closer to his age than mine. I frown at that thought.

Placing my hand on the small of her back, I guide her into the restaurant where I already have a reservation. The feeling of her soft flesh right underneath my fingertips is almost my undoing. My god, I want to skip dinner and take her straight home and pledge my undying love and devotion to her as I show her just how much she means to me.

And that's just it. I'm still practically a stranger to her, yet my soul has recognized its other half. I think it knew it that day on the beach, and that's why my gaze had been so drawn to her. I'd risk my life to save her a thousand times over if only for the simple fact that I feel like I'll cease to exist in a world where she doesn't exist.

That's why I haven't been able to forget about her since that day. That's why I've dreamed about her every night and shamelessly jacked my cock to visions of her in that pretty little bikini.

Oh, she's gorgeous, no doubt, with a sexy little body, but this is more than just simple lust.

I don't just want to fuck her body. I want to fuck her mind, her soul. I want to possess her and make her mine in every way.

These are feelings I've never had before, and I know they're not going away. This is it. She is it for me.

I just have to get her to see that too.

She's so wary of me, like a frightened doe ready to bolt at any moment.

I seat her, allowing my hand to trail up her back and over her bare shoulder before I reluctantly stop touching her and move to take my own seat across from her.

I know I should probably turn it down a notch, but I don't think I can.

When the waiter comes and offers to start us off with a bottle of wine, I ask for their best chardonnay. I know she's not legally old enough to drink yet, but no one here is going to ask to see her ID—especially since she's with me.

"Are you hungry?" I ask her, noting how thin her frame is. She seems even thinner than that day on the beach, like she hasn't been eating enough. I plan on rectifying that.

She nods and looks down at the menu in front of her before admitting, "I have no clue what to order, though. I've never been anywhere this fancy before."

She bites her lower lip at that last admission, and I have to fight back a groan. I want to leap across the table and nibble on its plushness myself, but somehow I restrain myself.

When the waiter comes back, I order us a sampler, and then I turn my full attention back to her.

She's still looking at me a bit warily, but she seems to have relaxed a bit since we're in public together.

"Are you going to tell me why you insisted I have dinner with you?" she asks and then stares at me expectantly.

Fair enough. She's letting me know she knows what I did with not really giving her a chance to decline my dinner offer.

I take a sip of my wine and motion for her to do the same. My fingers tighten around the stem of my glass as I watch her lips part and the yellow liquid flow between them as she takes a tiny sip.

She doesn't grimace like a first-timer, and I wonder if she's been wined and dined before. The thought comes with such a potent rush of jealousy that I ball my fist in my lap.

I do my best to brush it off as I answer her, "I haven't stopped thinking of you since that day I breathed life into your lungs."

I watch her still and then set her wine glass down gently.

"I've been kicking myself for not getting your name or number," I tell her honestly. "All those tortuous weeks of wanting to know more about you, yet I didn't have the first clue of where to look for you."

Her tiny brow furrows. "But you left before I could even thank you for saving me."

"I know," I reach across the table and grip her tiny hand in mine. "A decision that I've regretted every day since."

She stares down at our joined hands before she looks back up at me questioningly. "Why did you leave?"

I sigh and sit back in my chair. "Because when the EMTs arrived I knew you'd be in good hands. And I didn't want to be praised for being a hero."

I level a look at her. "Make no mistake, sweet Chloe. I may be a doctor, but I am no hero."

"But you save lives every day," she tells me gently.

"You help people. There's nothing more heroic than that."

Her baby blue eyes are big and shining, and she's looking at me so trustingly now with near worship in her eyes. I feel uncomfortable under her praise. I don't deserve it. "I'm just doing my job," I deflect. "And I don't save them all, Chloe. Try as I might, I can't save them all."

My mind goes back to my mom and how I couldn't save her. The one person I should have been a hero for, and I wasn't.

"But you try," she insists. "That in and of itself speaks volumes."

The way my chest tightens almost painfully when I look at her purity speaks volumes too. I want her like I've never wanted anything in my entire life.

Our food arrives, and we begin eating in silence. There's so much more I want to say to her, but she's eating pretty well, and I don't want to take her attention away from feeding herself. The girl's eating like she's starved. When was the last time she had a decent meal?

She lives in a nice little house and has a decent job at the hospital. I don't know what her story is, but I'm determined to find out.

She looks up from taking a bite to find me watching her.

"What?" she asks self-consciously.

My mouth tips up as I grin at her indulgently. "Nothing. I just enjoy watching you eat."

Her cheeks color at that, and she dabs her lips with a napkin. "Oh god, I'm sorry. I've been making a pig out of myself."

"Not at all," I motion to the table. "Eat as much as you want. Have you not been eating regularly?" I ask her clinically.

She hesitates before confessing, "Not really."

"Why not?" I ask her, making sure to use my best clinical bedside manner.

"Um, well, not since..." she hesitates again before taking a deep breath and going on, "not since my mom died earlier this year."

She looks so sad and lost I want to fold her into my arms. If anyone understands the pain of losing a mother, it's me.

"How did she die?" I ask her.

She squirms in her chair and shakes her head, her eyes dropping down to the table. "I'd really rather not talk about it," she mumbles.

Too soon. I get that too. "I get it. That's fine," I tell her.

She peeks up at me from under long lashes. Jesus, what I'd give to see her looking up at me like that from down on her knees with my cock between her sweet lips.

Fuuuck, focus Kevin.

"My mom died too," I tell her.

Her head snaps up and her eyes widen before they soften with empathy. "I'm sorry," she says.

I take another sip of my wine, still holding her gaze. "It was a long time ago. I was still a boy."

She doesn't ask how she died, but I tell her anyway. "She died of amiodarone toxicity."

"Amiodarone?" she repeats the term questioningly.

"It's a drug used to treat heart arrhythmia. My mother had aFib really bad. She took beta blockers for years until they stopped working. The doctors told her they could try this different type of medication or get an ablation. She opted for the medication rather than undergoing surgery."

Chloe's big eyes still haven't left me, so I plunge onward with my story. "She figured the medication would be safer than going under the knife—and normally it would have been. But, she was supposed to have been monitored for adverse side effects, and she never was. Her breathing started getting worse, and every time she called her doctor, he was out of town.

The nurses told her to stay on the medication until she could see him."

"But she never did," Chloe surmised softly.

I shake my head, my jaw clenching with fury even after all this time. "No, she ended up being rushed to the emergency room after months of taking the medication. She was struggling to breathe. They did a bronchoscopy and determined that the amdiodarone had damaged her lungs. It was a very rare side effect of the drug but one that would have been caught early on if she'd been properly monitored in the first two weeks of being given it."

Chloe's eyes are big and attentive, and I let out a breath before going on. "She was given steroids for treatment, but after the bronchoscopy, her oxygen levels never came back up. She was eventually put on a ventilator, and she never came off it. Her heart gave out on her during the fight to heal her lungs."

"How old were you when she died?" Chloe asks softly.

"Sixteen," I answer back, the old guilt creeping back in.

"There was nothing you could have done," Chloe tells me gently, as if sensing the direction of my thoughts.

I shake my head. "Yes, there is. I should have

researched the side effects myself. I should have insisted she find another doctor. I should have done so many things, Chloe. But I didn't. I failed her. The one person I really should have saved, I didn't. So you see, that's why I'll never be okay with being called a hero. Because I'm not."

"Is that why you became a doctor?" she asks me. "Because you wanted to help save other people since you couldn't save your mom?"

I nod tightly. "I didn't find out any of that stuff about side effects and all that until it was too late. Her doctor never advised her on any of it. I wanted to keep that from happening to someone else. I vowed that I would be a different kind of doctor. One who was truly invested in his patients and wouldn't just treat them like another statistic. "

Although it's still painful to think about, it feels good to share all of it with someone.

I let out another breath and sit back in my chair. "Jesus, I've never told anybody that," I tell her.

She gives me a tiny smile but then looks uncomfortable like maybe since I shared my story with her she's obligated to share hers too.

I quickly dispel that notion when I abruptly change the subject to lighten the atmosphere.

"Do you want any dessert?"

She blinks, processing my question before shaking her head. "Oh no, thank you. I couldn't eat another bite."

I pay the check, eager to get out of there and have her all to myself.

CHAPTER FOUR

Chloe

I DON'T KNOW if it's because of what Kevin shares with me about his mom's death or the way he seems to look right through me into my soul, but I feel more connected to him than anyone else I've ever met other than my mom.

And that's a problem.

He steers me outside with a palm against my back again. It doesn't go unnoticed by me how his hand nearly spans my entire back or how his fingers seem to tighten against my skin as we walk out of the door of the restaurant.

I look up at him. He's breathtakingly handsome in slacks and a button-up shirt with his hair swept carelessly back and his jaw clean-shaven. He catches me gazing at him and gives me a lopsided grin that makes my heart stutter within my chest in its own arrhythmia.

He helps me into the car like the perfect gentleman he is before he walks around to the driver's side and retrieves the keys from the valet, no doubt leaving him a generous tip if the delighted look on the guy's face is any indication.

Kevin turns to face me, his golden eyes pinning me in their hypnotic stare before he puts the car into drive. "Let me take you back to my place," he suggests, his eyes both smoldering and pleading.

I hesitate before answering. No good can come of this. I'm a virgin. I don't know the first thing about men other than what I've seen from my mother, and that's that they break your heart and leave you so depressed you'd do anything to escape the pain.

"I just want more time with you," he prods. "Nothing will happen that you don't want," he adds, gently coaxing me.

I swallow and shake my head. "I really don't think it's a good idea, Kevin."

Though I have to admit, I enjoyed dinner. I

enjoyed listening to him talk, watching him, learning his mannerisms, like how his biceps flex under his shirt with every movement.

I was humbled that he'd shared something with me he'd never shared with anyone else.

But I didn't ask for any of it. And it terrifies me. Why is he giving me all this? What does he want in return? Better yet, what will he do if he gets what he wants? Will he just discard me when he's done with me like my mom's last boyfriend did her? Will I end up like my mom? So heartbroken that I lose the will to live?

"Is there someone else?" the harshness of his voice breaks my reverie.

I stare at him in shock. His jaw is ticking, and he looks murderous at the thought.

He takes my silence as a yes.

"Get rid of him," he snaps before I even have a chance to say anything.

I shake my head, and his hands tighten on the steering wheel. "It's not like that."

If possible, his jaw hardens even more.

"What I mean is there is no one else. I mean, there's no one at all."

He relaxes fractionally. "Then what is it, Chloe?" he asks me.

"Please, just take me home," I beg softly, not wanting to explain anything more. How can I when I don't even fully understand it myself? I'd be lying if I said I wasn't attracted to him. Any hot-blooded woman would be.

I feel a strange aching between the apex of my things and press my legs together tightly, trying to ease it.

Something tells me Dr. Kevin Blake would have just the prescription for whatever is ailing me, but there's no way in hell we can go there.

He's too handsome, too rich, and I can totally see myself falling for him.

And if there's anything that my mother's death taught me, it's that love is dangerous. Like that Def Leppard song, love bites, and I'm not ready to bleed.

Kevin

It seems I can deny her nothing—even if what she's asking is to get away from me.

But I know I'm not imaging things. I don't think it's me she wants to get away from so much as whatever this strong connection between us is. I think it scares her, and I don't know why, and I think that's what she's really running from.

I don't believe for a second that this attraction is entirely one-sided. Yes, she's wary of me but not because she truly believes I'll hurt her—not physically at least.

I felt the way her body trembled under my touch when our skin met tonight. I saw the way she looked at me when she thought I wasn't looking. The way she clenched those pretty little legs of hers together in the seat over there.

My cock throbbed in response at the sight.

As much as I want to kidnap her and take her home and stuff her full of my cock, I'm going to honor her request.

But not before I make damn sure she remembers me and that she knows I'm not going anywhere.

We don't speak as I drive her to her house, but the energy pulsing between us is a live thing. It's thick with sexual tension, but it's more than that too. It's the sound of our souls reaching out and pulsing in tune with one another.

Chloe is my other half, and there's no way I'm ever letting her go now that I've found her.

I park on the side of the street in front of her house

and walk her to her door, my hand on the small of her back again—any excuse to touch her.

When we finally get to her front door, she turns to me with a nervous smile. "Thank you for dinner. I had a—"

I finally break. I don't let her finish her cliche letdown. I grasp her face in both of my hands and smash my lips to hers.

God, I've been dying to taste her, and she tastes even sweeter than I imagined. Like vanilla and brown sugar. She's decadent.

I suck on that bottom lip that she likes to bite so much before I groan and nibble gently on it, testing its fullness.

She whimpers, and that fucking sound only fuels my desire.

Arousal shoots straight to my groin until I feel the head of my erection pushing up against the zipper of my slacks.

I push my hands into her hair, shaking the pins loose. I want to feel it running through my fingers.

The long length glides through my fingers like silk, and I get a waft of the flowery shampoo she uses as it tumbles down around us.

I'm fucking high on the scent. I breathe her in

deeply, sucking her essence into my lungs like a nicotine-deprived smoker.

Her hands come up to rest lightly on my chest, and I wrap my arms around her, pulling her flush against me until my erection is pressing up into her stomach.

I angle her head back so that I can more fully plunder her mouth, stroking her tongue with mine.

My arms tighten around her triumphantly when I feel her tongue begin to tentatively mate with mine.

"Jesus, Chloe," I breathe against her lips when she finally pulls away from me long enough to gasp for air. "Don't send me away." I'll get on my hands and knees and beg her if she wants me to.

"I—" she chews on her bottom lip indecisively, and I growl, watching her worry it between her teeth. I hardly dare to hope that she's going to give in tonight. "I can't," she finally finishes with an apologetic look up at me. "I'm sorry."

"It doesn't matter," I tell her, and she looks up at me with wide eyes like maybe she's afraid she angered me or something. But, no, far from it.

I cup her cheek and set her mind at ease, "You're mine, Chloe Danes. Every little fucking thing about you was made for me. I know you feel it too. I don't know what's going on in that pretty little head of yours or why you're fighting this so much, but just know that in the end, you'll be with me. I'll be right here waiting for when you decide to accept that."

I give her a sound kiss, tasting that full bottom lip again before I make myself pull back from her.

Her eyes are as big as saucers as she stares up at me, speechless. I smile down at her, my heart filled with tenderness and a protective fire for this beautiful woman. *My* woman. "Goodnight, sweetheart," I tell her before I make myself walk back to my car so I don't give into the urge to haul her home with me right now.

God knows I don't want to be parted from her, but I'll wait as long as it fucking takes to convince her that she's mine.

***

Chloe

Holy fucking moly. My head keeps replaying the entire evening with Kevin. The intense way he looked at me. How he touched me so possessively. The things he said. The way he kissed me.

Jesus, the way he kissed me...I've never been kissed like that before. Sure, I've kissed a couple of high school boyfriends before, but their kisses had never been like *that*.

That was the kiss of a *man*—not a *boy*.

A man who knows exactly what he wants, and what he wants is me. He told me so.

While the knowledge fills my stomach with warmth and butterflies, it also scares the hell out of me and makes me a nervous ball of anxiety.

I can't let him get into my head.

I can't let a man have that kind of power over me. The kind of power Rex had had over my mom. Right before he stomped on her heart by cheating on her with another woman, driving her to commit suicide and leave me all alone.

I chew on my lip as I think. But maybe Kevin's not like that? A huge part of me wants to believe that. He's a doctor. He's committed to helping people—not hurting them. That part of him is genuine. I could tell when he was talking about his mother and how that had prompted him to go into medicine that he was passionate about what he said. My heart broke for him hearing his story of watching his mom die from medicine toxicity—something that should have been entirely avoidable.

His drive to change the world because of something bad that happened to his mother was admirable, and that's something we have in common. I want to go into mental health because of what happened to my mom, to help keep it from happening to someone else's mother.

Tears clog my throat when I think of how I found her passed out on her bed overdosed on pills. It'd been intentional. She simply didn't want to go on after Rex betrayed her.

I remember how charming Rex had been, how nice I'd always thought he was. I'd truly believed he'd loved my mom. I'd been happy for her.

But in the end, he'd cheated on her, and she couldn't take it. Whether he'd done it intentionally or not, the result was still the same.

You can never know for sure about someone.

That's why I have to stay away from Kevin Blake.

It'll only lead to heartbreak.

CHAPTER FIVE

Chloe

I GO to work the next day to find a huge arrangement of flowers on my desk.

Martha grins at me widely as she teases, "Looks like somebody's got an admirer."

My cheeks heat as I give her a polite smile and snatch the card from the arrangement, already knowing who it's from.

Have dinner with me again tonight. Pick you up at seven again. - Kevin

I huff out a sigh of frustration and look around the

lobby as if I can conjure him up on my annoyance alone.

I'd bet my last dollar I won't see the stubborn surgeon at all day. He'll be avoiding me to keep from giving me a chance to decline his invitation.

I consider marching through the hospital to find him, but I don't know if he's in surgeries today or where to even begin looking for him. Plus, I'm kept busy at the desk, answering phones and intaking patients.

I fume about his audacity on and off all day, though. I try to push him from my mind, but the sweet scent of the flowers keeps drawing my gaze to them and my mind, consequently, to him.

Which I'm sure was the whole point of the damn bouquet to begin with. He wants to imprint himself in my mind so I have no escape from him. Didn't he tell me in no uncertain terms that I would eventually be his?

Indignation rises up within me the more I think about it. Who does he think he is just ordering me to dinner and putting a claim on me like he owns me? He might have saved my life, but that doesn't automatically make me his.

No matter that he looks like a god with his perfectly chiseled face and tall frame that fits his clothes oh so perfectly. Or the way his amber eyes seem to glow with a fire all their own.

I make up my mind then and there that just because he tells me to have dinner with him again doesn't mean that I will.

That's why when he shows up at my house—early again no less—I'm dressed in yoga pants and a slouchy off the shoulder shirt with my hair up in a messy bun. Just like I would be if I were just lounging around the house—which I am.

He looks totally unsurprised to see me dressed in lounge clothes, and still he tells me, "You look beautiful."

I snort and cross my arms. I know I'm anything but. I look like a mess, which was the whole point.

"I don't feel like going out tonight," I tell him.

His eyes darken as his gaze roves over me in a way that makes me feel like maybe he can see right through my clothes.

"So we'll eat in." He pushes past me into my house uninvited, and I stand there in the doorway gaping after him like a fish.

"Kevin, you can't just—" I begin, but he silences me just like he did last night.

With a hand on either side of my face and his lips crashing down onto mine.

His tongue licks at the seam of my lips, and I open willingly to his exploration.

His tongue snakes into my mouth and twines with mine in a dance that makes my knees go weak.

What was I saying? Something about he couldn't do something?

He's sucking on my bottom lip now, and I can't think straight. My brain is misfiring. All my signals are being sent throughout my body in tingles.

"I've been waiting all damn day to do that," he growls as he finally pulls back from me, and I stare up at him dazedly.

There's no denying it. The man is a good kisser. He can kiss a girl stupid, which he's apparently done to me because I still can't think, much less talk.

"What are you in the mood for?" he asks me.

I shake my head as if trying to clear it of the magical fog that's descended over me at his kiss. "What?" I ask him.

He smirks down at me smugly like he knows the effect that kiss had on me. "To eat?"

"Kevin, I—" I begin, but he interrupts me again.

"You have to eat, Chloe."

"But I—" I begin again.

He suddenly pulls me flush against him. "Let me take care of you," he says in a rush, his hands tightening behind my back and locking me up against him. He's hard all over, especially down *there*. I feel my cheeks flaming at the knowledge that he wants me that badly.

I fight for control, though, pushing hard against his chest until he releases me, but only marginally. He allows me to put some space between our bodies, but his arms are still loped loosely around my waist.

"God, do you always interrupt people and steamroll over them like this?" I scowl up at him.

"Never," he tells me seriously before his gaze softens. "Just you, when I know what's best for you and am trying to keep you from talking yourself out of it."

I open my mouth to speak and nothing comes out. I close my mouth and stare up at him. God, that's exactly what I've been doing. How does he read me so well?

"It's because you're mine. We were made for each other."

I start to wonder if I spoke my thoughts aloud, but his lips twitch, and he cups my cheek in his big palm as he tells me, "Your face is an open book. I can read everything you're thinking on it."

I look down, the intensity of his eyes disarming. I'm drowning. Drowning in this...whatever this is. This pull that exists between us.

"Don't fight this," he whispers. "I know you feel it too, Chloe." He sucks in a shaky breath, dropping his forehead to mine and breathing out, "My god, I've waited my whole life to feel like this."

"Like what?" I whisper back.

"Like I've finally found the other half of my soul."

My knees weaken at his words, spoken like they were ripped from deep inside his spirit. He's not lying. He really feels that way.

I do too…

But…

As if he can sense my warring thoughts in my head again, he pulls back and tilts my head up, forcing me to meet his eyes.

My god, his golden gaze is hypnotic. He's like Kaa, that snake off *The Jungle Book*. When he holds me in his gaze like this, I'm entranced. All my worries seem to vanish.

My eyes flick down to his lips, and I unconsciously lick my own.

His eyes darken in response, and he lets out a strangled sound before his lips are descending upon mine again.

This kiss is tender and restrained while somehow still devouring my soul. It promises more, and when I feel Kevin's hands begin to slip down my sides to pull me flush against him, I don't even try to fight it this time.

Maybe I can enjoy this. Enjoy his kisses and touches without losing myself completely in him.

He begins kissing along my jawline and down the column of my throat. I let my head fall back, granting him greater access to my flesh. His lips are sinful, branding me everywhere they touch with his heat.

And then suddenly I feel his fingers stroking me through the fabric of my yoga pants, and I whimper at the sensation, the little pops of electricity that shoot between my thighs.

"Jesus, you're so fucking wet, baby. Soaked right through your little pants," he growls against my ear.

My instinct is to be embarrassed, but one look at his face and the fire blazing in his eyes, and I know that he likes my body's response to him.

His nostrils flare, and he begins breathing more heavily as he drops to his knees.

I stare down at him in surprise. "What are you—" I start to ask, but then he yanks my pants and panties down to my knees in one smooth motion before burying his face between my legs.

My face burns as I hear him inhaling deeply, scenting me, and then I lose all cognizant thought as I feel him kiss me wetly.

Oh. My. God. He's kissing me *there*. Where no one has ever even touched or seen before.

His tongue strokes me in long, firm licks. "Sweetest damn thing I've ever tasted," he growls against my sensitive mound before his tongue finds my nub and begins polishing it with his tongue in strong, circular strokes that have me fisting my hands in his hair.

Oh god, I don't know what's happening. The electric zaps between my legs are intensifying, and I think...I think I'm going to...

It's as if he can read my thoughts because he encourages me, "Let go, baby. Give me everything."

"I...I..." I pant, struggling to find words.

His mouth suddenly latches onto the little nub, sucking it rhythmically, and that's when I feel myself tumble over the edge.

My sex pulses and spasms, gripping at air, as white hot pleasure rolls throughout my entire body. My legs turn to jelly. I think I'm going to collapse, but then he's standing, scooping me up into his arms and carrying me through my house to my bedroom where he lays me down gently on my bed.

He lays down next to me and pulls me against him, stroking my hair, soothing me.

I'm languid in his arms, still coming down from my first-ever orgasm—a mind-shattering one at that.

"I never thought it would feel like that," I hear myself admit against his chest.

His hand stills on my hair, and I feel him pull back to look down at me.

The look on his face is incredulous. "Are you telling me that was your first orgasm?"

My cheeks flame, and I suddenly regret telling him. "I'm sorry I'm not experienced or anything," I try to look away from him in embarrassment, but he lets out a soft laugh and turns my head back to him.

"Thank fuck," he says. "It's been driving me crazy thinking of another man touching you."

I search his eyes.

"You're perfect," he reaffirms, his voice coming out husky. "I'm glad you waited for me."

Was that what I had been doing? Waiting for the right person? Waiting for him?

He leans down and kisses me again, and I feel that hard part of him pressing into me.

His pauses just long enough to pull my shirt off and then gazes down at my hardened nipples. They feel full and aching, but then he brushes the pads of his thumbs over them, and I arch up into him instinctively.

"So responsive," he groans before lowering his

head to suckle my breast, sending a rush of wetness straight to my swollen, sensitive sex.

I gasp at the sensation, and then I'm aching down there again, but he doesn't leave me wanting.

His hand moves between my legs, and I feel his fingers separating my folds, probing between them.

I tense at the foreign sensation, but he kisses me deeply, relaxing me as he pushes first one, then two fingers into me, stretching me.

His thumb is pressing against my clit as he does it, giving me a confusing sensation of pleasure and fullness that has me clinging to him, my nails digging into his back.

He seems to love every minute of it if the way he's looking down at me with hooded eyes is any indication.

I don't know where my bravery comes from, but suddenly I want to feel him too. I move my hand between us to tentatively grip the heavy length of him through his pants, and he sucks in a sharp breath at the touch.

My eyes widen when I feel the length and girth of him. I only have a moment to wrap my palm around him before he suddenly jerks back and yanks his shirt hurriedly over his head. Then, he releases himself from his pants.

I watch in fascination and not a little bit of fear as the huge member between his legs bobs out as he shucks off his pants. I barely have time to register his washboard abs and the muscular cut of his body because my eyes are frozen on the monster between his legs.

He's going to try to put *that* inside me?

I might be a virgin, but I know the basics of how sex is supposed to work, and I already know that his cock looks much too large to fit in my tiny, unbreached hole.

As if sensing my worry, he gently drops back down on top of me and begins kissing me deeply again. I feel myself relaxing into the kiss, and then we're pressed against each other, naked flesh against naked flesh, all his hardness pressed against my softness.

His cock is prodding me between the legs, and then I feel him sliding up and down between my wetness, lubricating the head.

I tense, but then I feel Kevin's hands on either side of my face.

I look up into his eyes, and my breath catches at the possessive yet tender way he's looking down at me. "I want to look at you when I make you mine," he whispers. "Don't take your eyes off mine, sweet Chloe."

I swallow and do as he says, mesmerized by the hypnotic power of his gaze.

I feel him pushing into me, and I gasp at the uncomfortable stretch and burn, the increasing pressure of his thick sex impaling me.

My breathing becomes more shallow, and I reflexively close my eyes.

"Eyes on me, baby," he croaks out as if he too is in pain.

My eyes snap back open, and his are blazing down into mine with a hungry light. His breathing has become more ragged with the effort of holding back. His jaw clenches as he continues looking down into my eyes, and then he gives one final, hard push, and I feel my feminine barrier give way.

I cry out and he groans as he slips deep inside me, our eyes locked together the whole time.

We stare at each other for a moment, both breathing heavily. It's like he's invaded more than just my body. With our eyes locked like this, he's slipped inside my heart, my mind, my soul.

I've never felt so connected to another person as I do now. We're sharing the same breaths, the same heartbeat. I already know that this is so much more than just simple sex.

This is two people becoming one, two souls joining

together, and I know now that I don't have the power to fight this pull between Kevin and me.

It's too strong. Too primal.

He leans down and kisses me deeply, growling into my mouth, and I know he feels it too.

And then he begins to move within me, slowly at first, stroking in and out of me in long, slow strokes that send pleasure rippling throughout my core.

I cling to him as his thrusts pick up tempo. He's holding me clasped tight against him, chest to chest as he slams in and out of me, filling me over and over again.

"Kevin!" I whine his name as the tingling sensation grows and begins to expand.

"Oh god, fuck, Chloe. I can't stop. I can't stop." He's grunting into my neck, his breathing labored. "Come with me, baby. Let me feel that little pussy pulsing around me."

His desperate words combined with a hard, deep jab are my undoing. My legs shake as I cry out with the force of my orgasm. The first one he gave me when he licked me was more of an outward ripple. This one is deep and shakes me from within, causing my limbs to tremble and my breath to hitch with its intensity.

He lets out a guttural sound, and then I feel the

hot jets of his seed spraying deep inside me, filling me up with liquid warmth.

He continues pumping in jerky movements until he's completely emptied himself inside me, and I feel him leaking out.

I'm nothing but mush in his arms, all liquid limbs incapable of movement.

That's okay, though, because without pulling out of me, he rolls us onto our sides and scoops me up against him, kissing my hair and forehead as he tells me how perfect I am.

"I'm never going to let you go now, Chloe," he says.

A warm glow of belonging falls over me, and I dare to believe him.

CHAPTER SIX

Kevin

LAST NIGHT WAS the best night of my life. I held Chloe close in my arms all night. Although I wanted to make love to her again and again, I didn't, sensing her body needed rest after the first time. I know she was sore, and I never want to hurt her.

Instead, I held her. She let me pet her and stroke her all over her body as we talked late into the night.

I still couldn't get her to open up completely about what happened to her mother, but she shared some good memories about her with me, which was progress.

I'll take whatever I could get.

My world is finally complete. It's like a puzzle piece has snapped into place. One that I didn't realize I was missing until I found it.

Chloe is what I've been missing, and she fits so perfectly in my world.

I still love my job, but now I'm actually looking forward to getting off work so that I can spend more time with her: my woman.

My woman. A surge of possessive lust runs through me again when I remember taking her, knowing that I was the first and only man to ever be inside her. She's mine. Completely. Indefinitely. And I'm insanely, obsessively pleased by that fact.

No other man's touch will ever sit between us. Mine is the only one she'll ever know. I've never had a thing for virgins before, but with Chloe, I want it all. I want to be her first, her last, her only, her everything.

I drove us to work together that morning despite Chloe's halfhearted protestations. I don't want to let her out of my sight any more than she has to be.

She's mine. Mine to take care of. Mine to protect. Mine to love.

Mine, mine, mine.

Claiming her in the most primal way has only fueled my obsession with her. I know that I'll never get enough of her now.

She is my everything. I will give her anything her heart desires, my last breath if that's what she wants.

Speaking of my everything...

I walk out into the lobby and see her sitting at her desk with her back to me.

I stand there for a moment, enjoying the way her hair shimmers when she flicks a long strand over her shoulder.

Her fingers fly over the keyboard as she types up something.

She's interrupted when one of the male nurses comes out of the adjoining hallway and walks up to her with a shit-eating grin on his face.

"Chloe, babe," he greets her, and I frown, instinctively hating the way the little fucker is ogling her and the way he's speaking to her.

"Shawn, can I help you?" she asks him with a polite smile.

The four-headed beast of jealousy rises up within me at that smile. I realize she's just being polite, but it still knifes me to see her smiling at any other male. That's how far my fixation with her has gone. All her smiles are *mine*. *Mine*. She's mine.

I walk up behind her and place a hand on her shoulder. She starts and looks up at me with a genuine smile that reaches her eyes.

I'm partly mollified at the knowledge that the smile she gave me and the one she gave this little shit are totally different. She reserved her real smile for *me*.

I glare at the other male and see his eyes flick to where my hand is still resting on her shoulder familiarly. Take that fucker.

I realize I'm being territorial as fuck, but I don't give a shit. Chloe is mine, and if this fucking prick knows what's good for him, he'll get the fuck out of here before I break his bones for looking at my woman. I might be a doctor who took a Hippocratic oath to my patients, but I'm a man first—a man who's insanely possessive of what's his—and I won't hesitate to be the reason someone's admitted to the hospital if they make a move on my girl.

And apparently that's what the little fucker had in mind because suddenly he mumbles something about not really needing anything after all before he skulks away.

I'm already pulling Chloe out of the chair before he's even fully retreated down the hallway.

"Take your break now," I order her.

"But someone has to man the desk," she frowns.

"Martha!" I bark, and I see the woman's head pop up over the partition separating the reception desks.

"Yes, Dr. Blake?" she asks with a smile.

"Do you mind manning the floor on your own for a few minutes so Chloe can go ahead and take her break? There are some things I need to discuss with her."

Martha beams at us before nodding. "Of course not! You got it, Dr. Blake."

I grin down at a blushing Chloe before pulling her along with me.

"Kevin, where are you taking me?" she whispers as I drag her down the hallway.

I finally reach the deserted hallway I'm looking for and open the door to one of the unused offices.

I pull her inside and immediately back her up against the shut door, angling her head up to kiss her.

She's surprised, but then I feel her soften underneath me as she moans into my mouth, her arms wrapping around my neck.

"I've been wanting to do that for three fucking hours," I admit to her in between licks.

She giggles, but I smother the sound by devouring her mouth again.

Fuck. I'm hard. My cock is a rod of steel in my pants, and I know I won't be able to function until I have her again.

I lift her legs up and wrap them around me, needing to be inside her *now*.

I pull my pants down just enough to free my cock, and then I push her skirt up and pull her panties to the side.

"Kevin," she says my name breathlessly in my ear, and that sound—the sound of her panting my name—is nearly my undoing. Precum leaks from the tip of my cock, and I'm almost dizzy with lust when I line myself up against her sweet hole.

I feel her answering wetness dripping down onto me, and I breathe out a harsh breath. *Fuck.*

I try to be gentle as I push into her, but she's so fucking tight and hot and wet that I can't help slamming up into her hard.

"Fuck, baby, you're so perfect," I whisper against her lips.

She cries out at another deep thrust, and I capture her lips with mine to muffle the sound. No one should be back in this abandoned part of the hospital, but for just in case.

I'm only a few pumps in when I feel heat settling at the base of my spine and know I'm close.

I strain with the effort to hold back until I feel Chloe's cunt ripple around me.

"Yes, that's it, baby. Come all over my cock," I prompt her.

She does, her pussy gripping and milking me in

sucking pulses that send me toppling over the edge too. My balls churn, and then I feel the fiery rush of my seed up my length. I groan at the intense release of the pressure bursting gloriously through my head. I slam my cock as deep as it will go into her as I feel my member pulsing the biggest load of my life into her.

I slump against her, still holding her up against the door until I think I can function without toppling over.

I grab some tissues off the desk and help her clean herself up. As much as I love the thought of her walking around all day with my cum dripping down her legs, I came so much I know that'd be bound to make a mess.

"I should probably be getting back. We've been gone more than a few minutes," she tells me as grins up at me shyly.

I laugh. "Me too, baby. I don't have any surgeries scheduled today, but I've probably kept my latest appointment sitting in the waiting room long enough."

Chloe wraps her little arms around my neck and presses her face into my chest, cuddling up close to me.

"I'm really glad you're the one who saved me, Kevin," she tells me trustingly, and my chest tightens painfully.

Her trust is everything. *She* is everything.

I hold her close and vow to myself that I will never lose her.

<hr>

Chloe

I'm happy for the first time since Mom died. Of course, thoughts of how she died still fill me with that same sadness, but it's not as intense as before.

And that's because I have Kevin.

He came into my life like a shining beacon of hope. He wouldn't take no for an answer and successfully burrowed himself into my life and heart, proclaiming that now that he found me, he'd never let me go.

Maybe statements like that that border on obsession should scare me, but they simply reassure me. They make me feel better. Safe and secure.

For the past week, Kevin and I have been inseparable when we're off the clock. Even when we're at work, he oftentimes finds me and takes me to one of the unused rooms for a quickie. We divide the nights up between my house and his place. We don't really care where we are so long as we're together.

I've quickly come to depend on his presence, the warmth in his eyes. He's no longer on call except once a week. I think he used to stay on call all the time. He used to throw himself into work before me. When I mentioned something to him about not wanting to take him from his patients, he told me that he's learned that taking care of himself is important too if he wants to be able to offer the best to his patients. He proclaimed that spending time with me is what relaxes him and helps him get through each day.

I can't very well argue with that because I want him home more too.

Everything is going great, and I'm falling more and more in love with him every day.

But then one night I have a nightmare that shakes me so badly I'm catapulted back to those months right after Mom died.

I dream of her. I see her body laying out on her bed, the open pill bottle all around her just like I found her.

But in my nightmare, her lifeless hand reaches out and grasps mine before her lips move, warning me, "It will end in death." Although her lips move to deliver the words, her eyes are dead and glassy.

I bolt upright in the bed and look around, panting. Kevin is lying next to me fast asleep, and I slip from the bed soundlessly so as not to wake him.

My hands are shaking with the aftereffects of the

nightmare. My heart is racing, and I can't calm my anxious thoughts.

What was that? A premonition telling me things can never work out between Kevin and me?

I shake my head. Kevin is nothing like Rex was, though. He loves me. He'd never hurt me.

But wasn't that what Mom believed about Rex?

I need air. Without really thinking about what I'm doing, I throw on my bikini and a cover up and quietly slip out of the door.

I walk the couple of blocks to the ocean and then stand on the shoreline staring out at the moonlight glinting off of the waves.

There's not another soul out here on the beach at this time of night.

My mind is swirling with possibilities. What would I do if Kevin betrayed me like Rex did Mom? If I found him with another woman, would I snap and go crazy like Mom did? Does suicide run in families? Maybe I'm cursed just like my mom and doomed to repeat her mistakes.

I'm deep in thought and begin walking out into the ocean, enjoying the rush of the pulling of the waves against my legs. Somehow the ocean always grounds me. Maybe I do have a bit of my mom in me. She always used to come to the ocean to think too.

"Chloe!" I'm snapped out of my thoughts when I hear Kevin screaming my name, the worry evident in his tone.

I turn and see him standing up on the shore in a pair of shorts he must have hastily thrown on before coming to find me.

"It's okay!" I yell back seeking to reassure him. "I'm fine—" I try to say, but then a huge wave comes out of nowhere and crashes over me, knocking me down.

I instantly panic. Oh god, not again. I haven't even come that far out. The water isn't even up to my shoulders.

The water is furious, though, and pulls me under, dragging me with it.

I try to swim up to the surface, but the more I fight against the current, the quicker I tire myself out.

This is it, I think. *The ocean is finally going to kill my stupid ass this time.*

But then I feel strong arms around me, and Kevin is hauling me up against his chest, swimming me into shallower water.

He gets us up to our knees before he turns around and crushes me to his chest, scolding me furiously. "What the fuck, Chloe? Are you trying to get yourself killed?"

Those words...the way they remind me of how mom killed herself...they're my undoing. The tears come in a rush, and sobs begin pouring out of me.

Kevin just pulls me tight against him again, his strong arms wrapping around me, holding me tightly, securely, as he works to soothe me. "Ssshh, it's okay. I've got you now. Everything's going to be alright."

My face is buried in his chest, and I feel him stoop to lift me up into his arms. He cradles me against him, and I let him.

He carries me back up to the safety of the shore before he sits on the sand, still cradling me in his lap.

"Chloe, talk to me," he begs me.

I look into his golden eyes, and suddenly I know that he's known this whole time that there's something I've been holding back from him.

He's given me everything. He told me about his mother. He's held nothing back, but I've been holding onto this secret desperately.

It's not fair.

So, I finally tell him everything that happened that night.

And it's cleansing, therapeutic, as if by speaking it all aloud I'm finally able to let it all go.

And Kevin being as in tune with me as he always is picks up on even what I don't say.

"And you were afraid that the same thing was going to happen between us?" he asks me gently.

I look at him cautiously and nod.

He lets out a sigh and shakes his head. "Chloe, let me make this perfectly clear. You are it for me. There will *never* be another woman for me. You're all I want. I was fucking obsessed with you before I ever even knew who you were. I love you," he tells me firmly.

Tears cloud my vision as I stare into his hypnotic gaze.

He wipes the tears from my eyes, and his voice gets husky as he admits, "If you ever killed yourself, I'd follow you into death. I can't live without you, baby. *That's* real love, and that's what I have for you. So no more doubts, okay? I'm so sorry for what happened to your mom, but you're not her, and I'm certainly not like that fuck-off she was with."

"I'm sorry," I whisper. How could I have ever compared him to Rex? I know deep in my bones that Kevin truly loves me, that he would do anything for me.

"Don't be sorry, Chloe." His lips hover just a breath away from mine. "Just be mine," he orders before he claims my lips in a soul-touching kiss that leaves no doubt in my mind exactly who I belong to.

EPILOGUE

Five Years Later

Kevin

"I'M HERE to see Mrs. Blake," I tell the receptionist at the mental health center.

She gives me a toothy grin. "Of course, Mr. Blake. I'll let her know you're here."

I smile back at the woman and remain standing as she goes to collect my wife.

My *wife*.

It feels so good to call her that.

Chloe and I have been married for going on five

years now. After she fully opened up to me that night on the beach, I couldn't wait to make her mine in every way.

We had a small ceremony on the patch of the beach where I saved her life. It was just the two of us and a couple of witnesses. Chloe doesn't have much family to speak of, and neither do I, but we have each other—and our two kids—and that's all that matters.

Justin was born almost exactly nine months after the first time I ever slept with her. In hindsight, I think that subconsciously I didn't use protection with Chloe on purpose, whether I realized it myself at the time or not. I think I'd been determined to tie her to me in every way possible. That probably makes me a bastard, but we're together, and she's happy, and I'm happy, so so be it.

A year after Justin was born, we had Molly. Both of our children have their mother's stunning blonde hair, but they've both got my golden eyes. Sometimes I wish they had Chloe's baby blue eyes, but she says she loves their golden eyes, and if she's happy, then I'm happy.

My eyes scan my wife's practice, and my chest swells with pride. Shortly after we got married, Chloe got her B.S. in behavioral science and started her own mental health practice where she counsels people going through bad breakups and other life crises. She runs a suicide hotline, determined to be the voice of reason for anyone thinking of taking their own life, and she and her team have saved countless lives.

I glance down at my watch. We still have a couple of hours before we have to relieve the nanny, and while I love the kids and can't wait to see them, I need some time alone with my wife.

She finally comes out of the back, looking radiant in a pair of high heels, a pencil skirt, and a button-up blouse. She's got her hair twisted up in a professional bun, though, and that'll be the first thing to go once I get her alone.

"Dr. Blake," she grins at me coyly.

"Mrs. Blake," I take her hand and begin leading her out the door to my waiting car.

"Where are you taking me, husband?" she asks curiously.

I shoot her a look filled with heat and smirk at her. "You'll see."

She bites her lip, and I feel my already hard cock getting even harder in my pants.

Goddamn.

I finally pull up outside the little beach house. Although she moved into my place after we got married, we kept her beach bungalow too as a vacation spot and getaway. Plus, she could never get rid of that place where she'd grown up and had such fond memories with her mother, and I'd never ask her too.

Besides, this cottage serves its purposes.

I haul her through the door, my cock about to bust through my pants.

No sooner do I get the door closed than I have her pressed up against it.

Fuck, it's always like this. No matter how many times I have her, it's never enough. I'm always like a starving man at his last meal when it comes to my wife.

I yank at her shirt, too impatient to mess with the buttons. She gasps as it rips, and I feel a primitive sense of satisfaction at the sound. I push the cups of her lacy bra down to reveal her pink nipples, already hardened in anticipation of my mouth.

The sight excites me so much I feel a stream of precum ejaculate from the tip of my erection.

I latch onto her nipple, knowing what she likes.

Her head falls back against the door as her arms wrap around my head.

I lift her up until her legs wrap around my waist.

Jesus, I can feel her wetness through our clothes.

The evidence that she wants me just as badly as I want her always turns me into a beast.

I make good on my earlier promise to myself and

thrust my fingers into her hair, letting it down while I devour her mouth greedily, sucking on her tongue.

I can never get enough of her vanilla and brown sugar taste.

I haul her up against me and carry her to the bedroom where I turn her and position her on the bed on all fours.

Her eyes are hooded and lust-filled when she gazes back at me over her shoulder.

Fucking hell. Her in that position with her skirt pushed up around her waist, her shirt ripped, her tits falling out of her bra, and her pussy wet and dripping around her thong makes for the best kind of porn. I could take a picture of her just like this with that sexy look in her eyes and jerk off to it for a month.

"Kevin," she pants, "I'm feeling feverish."

I see the glint in her eyes and know she's feeling playful. I grin. "Yeah? Do you hurt anywhere?"

She bites her lip and nods.

"Where? Where does it hurt?" my voice comes out on a rasp.

"Right here," she moves her hand between her legs, and I make a strangled sound as I feel another jet of precum shoot out of my cock, making a mess of the inside of my slacks.

"What kind of hurt is it?" my voice is husky with insinuation.

"Throbbing," she whines.

Fuuuck. I've got to be inside her. *Now.*

"You're in luck," I tell her, my hands shaking with impatience as I yank down my pants, "because I've got just what the doctor ordered."

"Ah!" she cries out, her eyes rolling back in her head when I spear her with one hard thrust. Even after two kids and as often as I fuck her, she's still tight as a virgin, even more so from this position.

I'm so wound up from our foreplay that I'm only three pumps in when I feel myself getting ready to blow.

I reach down between her legs and rub her clit in circles, applying just the right amount of pressure to get her off in record time.

Her body recognizes its master and comes at my command, her pussy squelching as I continue to ride her through the waves of her orgasm, holding her up with a hand wrapped around her waist. I feel my own orgasm rising up within me and grunt out between clenched teeth, "Get ready for your medicine, baby," I drive into her until my own release shoots out of me in an explosive gush that nearly sends me to my knees.

She lets out a soft laugh as I place kisses along the

back of her neck. "I should let you treat me more often."

I grin against her neck. "Call me for a check-up anytime, baby."

THE END

Connect with Emma!

Visit Emma's website to get a FREE book you can't get anywhere else: www.authoremmabray.com.